Written by Jared Burgess
Illustrated by Metakomik
Cover Art by Metakomik

Published by Etched Mythos LLC
EtchedMythos.com
Find Us On Tiktok/Instagram at EtchedMythos

Issue #1   First Printing
Published 2026

For permissions inquiries: etchedmythos@gmail.com

MOVE FASTER!!!
WHUMMM...

PUSH HARDER!!!
PICK YOURSELF UP!!!

FWOOSH

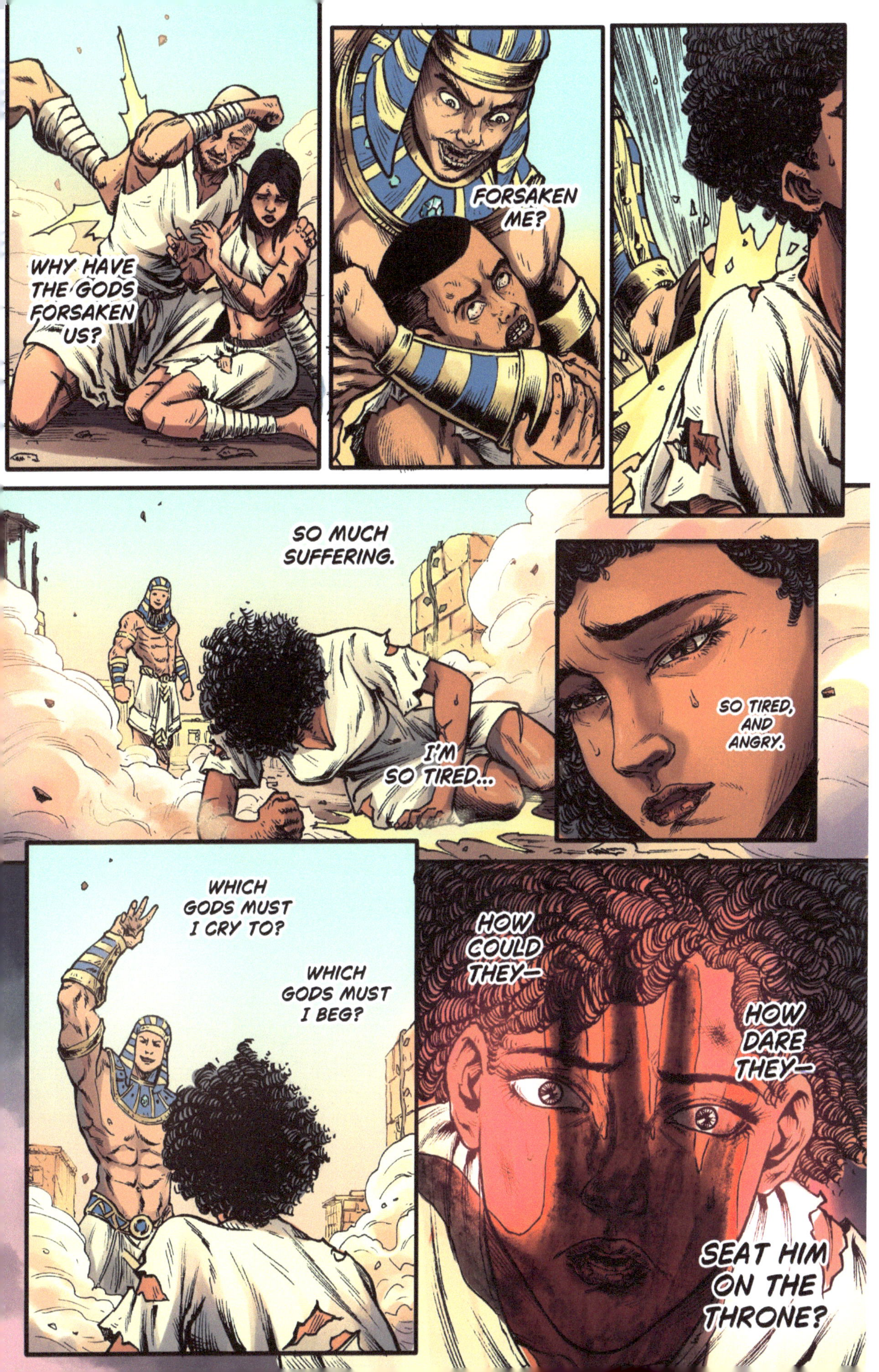

WHY HAVE THE GODS FORSAKEN US?
FORSAKEN ME?
SO MUCH SUFFERING.
I'M SO TIRED...
SO TIRED, AND ANGRY.
WHICH GODS MUST I CRY TO?
WHICH GODS MUST I BEG?
HOW COULD THEY—
HOW DARE THEY—
SEAT HIM ON THE THRONE?

A QUIET HUM SEEPS INTO THE AIR...
THE LIGHT BREATHES, ALIVE AND WATCHING.

THE HEAVENS RIPPLE, BLEEDING INTO SHADES OF FIRE.
THE WORLD GROANS AS GOLD DROWNS IN CRIMSON.

ALL IS SWALLOWED IN A FLOOD OF RED.

TIME ITSELF PAUSES BENEATH THE SCARLET VEIL.

THE GLOW COLLAPSES IN ON ITSELF—GONE. SILENCE RUSHES BACK, HEAVIER THAN SOUND.

ONLY BREATH...

AND A SINGLE TEAR REMAIN.

WHO TOLD YOU TO STOP!?
WHOOSH—
I WON'T TELL YOU AGAIN, KHETEMU (SLAVE).
FUHHSH
HUH?
SSHHHH

WHOOOSH

AAAA AAAA AGH!!!

HELP ME!!!
FWOOOSH

HELP HIM! QUICK!!

VVVRRRMM
SSSHHHH

AAAA AAAA AGH!!!
SSHHHH
FFRRNNNG

YOU!!!

FWIIIP
WHAT DID YOU DO TO HIM?!

BOOOM!!

KILL HER!!!

KROOSH!
SMACK!

THUMP!

THUD!

HEY!!!
KREEEAK...
THMP...
THMP...
CRSHHH!
KRKKK!
KRKKK!
KABOOOM!
GASP!
SHING!
WHMMMM!...
THMP-
THMP!

SHING!
ZOOOOOMM!!
SILENCE! YOU DARE DEFY YOUR MASTER? I WILL CRUSH THIS PATHETIC UPRISING!

CRACK! SNAP!
GAHK!!

THUD!
HOW... HOW YOU...

WHUMMMM...

IT'S OVER NOW.

FREEDOM!
YEAH WE'RE FREE!!!

MAYBE THIS WAS MA'AT'S PURPOSE FOR ME...

TO LEVEL THE FIELD.

TO TAKE THEIR PRIDE.

TO GIVE POWER...
TO THE POWERLESS.

TO SET THE ORDER RIGHT.
OR MAYBE...
TO HURT THOSE WHO THINK THEY'RE ABOVE.

ENOUGH OF THIS DEFIANCE.
ON YOUR KNEES, NOW!!!
WHRTMMM
WHRROOOMM!
GRRRAAKKK!
CRKKK...
CRKKK...

THUD!
SSSRRKK!
THWAAAK!
BOOOOM!!
AAHH~!
WHUMP...!
THUMP

!
SHING!
NO MORE.

STAND DOWN! NOW!

THOOM!
GET OFF OF HER!!!

PROTECT HER!!!
NO MORE CHAINS!!!

AAAAAAAAA
RRRGGGH!!
SHNK!!

ATTACK THEM!!!

NO...
WAIT-!!

BWHAM!

HAAAHH
HHH–

WHOOOOMMMM...

FSSSHH-WFF!

SHRAA
THWAAAK!

NO...
SHE'S HURT.

I... I'M FINE...
YOU'RE BLEEDING.

STAY AWAKE—LOOK AT ME.

FWOOSH...

THEY'LL COME AFTER US...
LET THEM. WE'RE NOT LOSING YOU.

HOLD ON. I'LL STOP THE BLEEDING.

RUSTLE
RUSTLE

HMM...
WHAT IS
THIS?

SSHHFF
SSHHFF

HOLD
STILL.

THIS
GONNA
HURT...

SSSSHHH—

KRRRK
K
K
SCRRRAAK

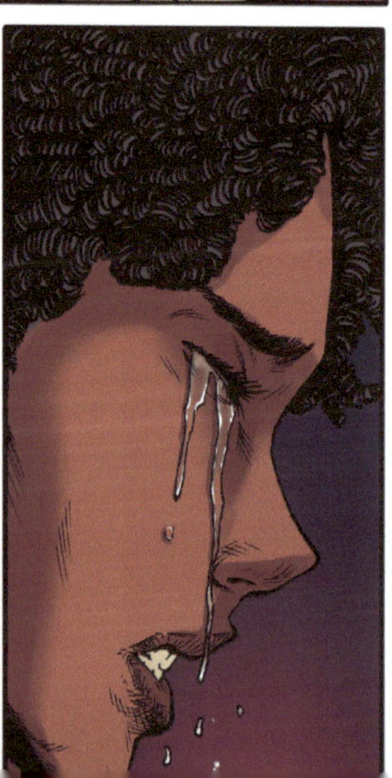

I KNOW THIS IS VERY PAINFUL.
BUT YOU'VE GOT SAND DEEP IN THESE CUTS... CAN'T LET IT STAY.

IF TODAY IS THE DAY... THEN SO BE IT

CLINK.
CLINK.

SHNK!!

HERE. HOLD IT TO YOUR BACK.

I NEED TO GIVE US A CHANCE.

I WON'T LET OTHERS FIGHT FOR MY FREEDOM WHILE I HIDE.

GRRNNT...
WHAT'S YOUR NAME, WOMAN?

THOSE PEOPLE OUT THERE, THEY'RE NOT JUST FIGHTING FOR YOU.
THEY'RE FIGHTING FOR ALL OF US.
AT THE END, THEY'LL NEED TO KNOW THE NAME OF THE WOMAN WHO LIT THE SPARKS INSIDE THEM.

SO I ASK AGAIN...
WHAT. IS. YOUR. NAME?
MY NAME IS RENETTA.

RENETTA.
MY LADY.

FOR AS LONG AS I BREATHE...
I, ANKHSET, SHALL BE YOUR SHIELD.

GATHER YOUR STRENGTH.
I'LL RETURN WITH SOLDIERS WHOSE FIRE BURNS HOTTER THAN SEKHMET'S BREATH.

AAAARGHH

THWAAAK!
THWAAAK!
THWAAAK!

GRRRAAKKK!

RIP
RIP
THEY TAUGHT ME...

NEVER TO SHOW WEAKNESS...

NEVER TO DREAM...
GRIP

AND NOW FREEDOM...

KRRK
IT COSTS BLOOD.

RUSTLE
WHICH GOD GAVE ME THIS?

THUD THUD
NUT? OSIRIS? RA?
FWOOOSH

HUFT...
ACTUALLY... IT DOESN'T MATTER. I HAVE IT-

-AND THEY DON'T.
FWOOOSH

FSSHHK

FWUMP

FLAP
FLAP

FWAAAAASSSHH

THWAAAK!
THWAAAK!
THWAAAK!
THWAAAK!
THWAAAK!

AAAARRGGHH

GRRDAKKKK!

SHNK!!
HUDDLE TOGETHER! BACK TO ME!

WHOOOMMMM

FWAAAAASSSHH
FLAP
FLAP

FWISHH!
KRAANG!
UGH!!
KRAAAGH!
AARGH!!
THWAAAK!
THUD!
WHUMMMMM...
GRRK...
TCH...

THEY'LL ASK
MY NAME.

BOTH
UPPER...

...AND LOWER EGYPT.

THEY'LL
REMEMBER.

AND THEY'LL
KNOW WHAT
HAPPENS...
WHEN A SLAVE
LEARNS POWER.

DESERT SLAVE ENCAMPMENT
– MIDDAY –
WHSP-
WHSP
SHFF...
SHFF...

THEY'RE CLOSING IN...

:TAP:

WHOOSH–

FWP

HA-HA-HA!
ARE YOU KIDDING ME?

SSHDHH

WHRRRRMM
AAAAAAAAA AAAAA!!!
BY THE GODS...
CRRRRRNNN
SCRRREEEEEK
I CAN'T MOVE— MY LEGS—!!!

KAA— THOOOM!!!

CRRRK...
RMMMBLE...
RMMMBLE...

I SHALL HONOR YOU AS THE ONE TRUE PHARAOH OF EGYPT.
FOR I HAVE SEEN THE POWERS AND WILL OF THE GODS IN YOU.
YOU ARE MY *PHARAOH*. MY PHARAOH *RENETTA*.
FOR AS LONG AS I LIVE, MY DEAR LADY...

MY PHARAOH RENETTA.

MY BROTHERS! MY SISTERS! I KNOW WHAT I'VE ENDURED. I KNOW WHAT YOU'VE ENDURED.
AND I SWEAR THIS— I AM DONE LIVING IN TREPIDATION!

THE NATURAL ORDER OF LIFE NO LONGER SEEMS NATURAL! OUR PAIN, OUR CRIES, OUR FAITH—
THEY HAVE *NOT* GONE *UNHEARD!*

SHHNK!
WE WERE TESTED.

WE PASSED.

AND IN RETURN...

...WE WERE GIVEN HER!

A GODDESS OF OUR OWN!

NOW WHAT'S OUR NEXT STEP,...
SOMEONE'S ON MY THRONE.
...MY PHARAOH?

TO BE CONTINUED IN ISSUE #2

The First Two Pages Are Next

CRACKLE
CRACKLE
CRACKLE
CRACKLE
CRACKLE
WHOOP
...
BEFORE THE NILE FLOWED, AND BEFORE THE FIRST MAN-MADE PYRAMID...
...THERE WAS OSIRIS.
TAP
ANOTHER GOD STORY?
LEARNING A BIT MORE OF OUR CULTURE WOULDN'T HURT FOR YOU.

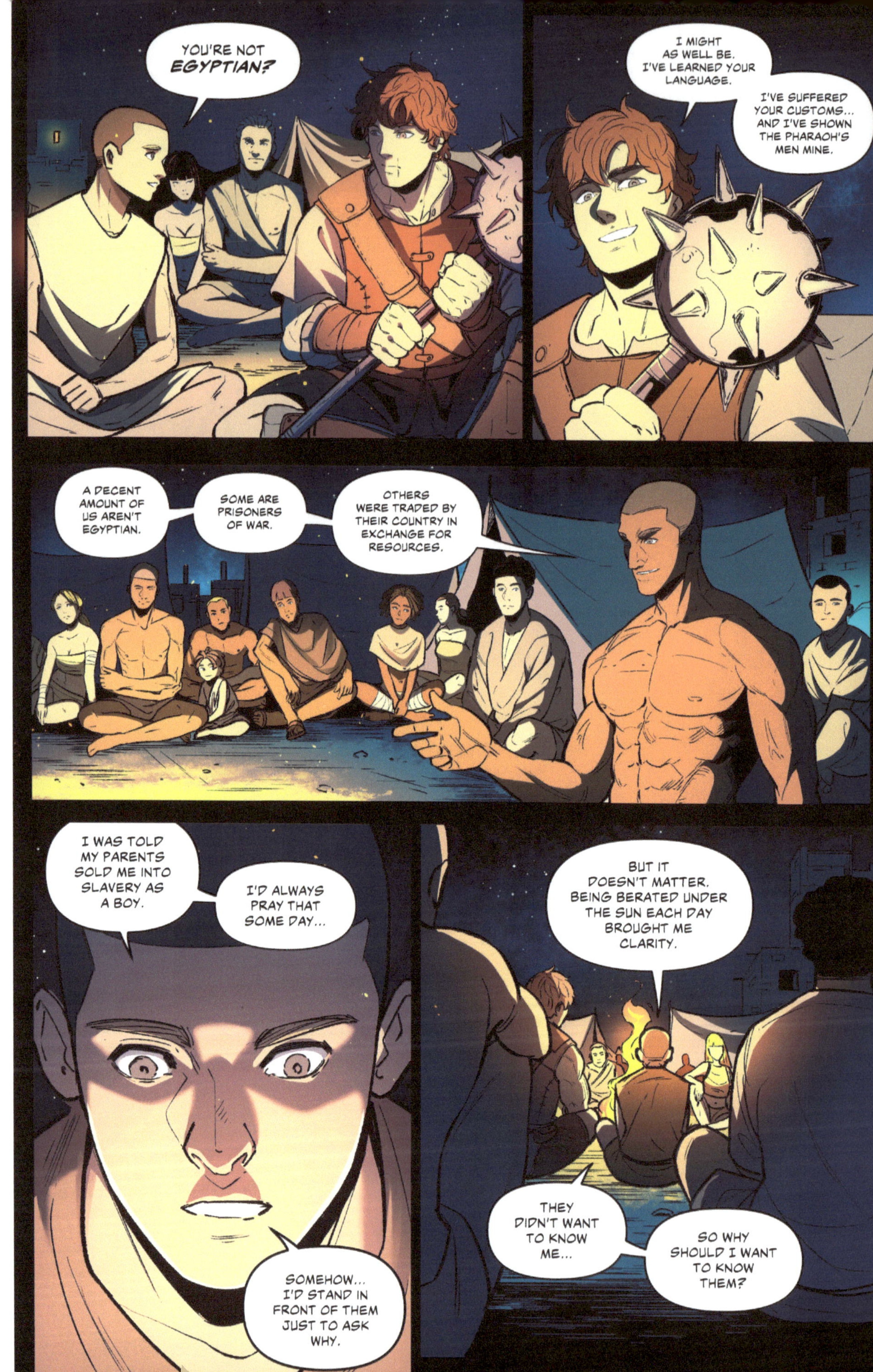

YOU'RE NOT EGYPTIAN?
I MIGHT AS WELL BE. I'VE LEARNED YOUR LANGUAGE.
I'VE SUFFERED YOUR CUSTOMS... AND I'VE SHOWN THE PHARAOH'S MEN MINE.
A DECENT AMOUNT OF US AREN'T EGYPTIAN.
SOME ARE PRISONERS OF WAR.
OTHERS WERE TRADED BY THEIR COUNTRY IN EXCHANGE FOR RESOURCES.
I WAS TOLD MY PARENTS SOLD ME INTO SLAVERY AS A BOY.
I'D ALWAYS PRAY THAT SOME DAY...
SOMEHOW... I'D STAND IN FRONT OF THEM JUST TO ASK WHY.
BUT IT DOESN'T MATTER. BEING BERATED UNDER THE SUN EACH DAY BROUGHT ME CLARITY.
THEY DIDN'T WANT TO KNOW ME...
SO WHY SHOULD I WANT TO KNOW THEM?

Enjoying the Story From the Graphic Novel?

Get the Full Story Sooner from the Book

The Powers of Ra!

Look for this Cover on Amazon or IngramSpark!

THE POWERS OF RA

From the Creator

My Name is Jared Burgess and This is my First Splash into the Comic World.

This Comic is Solely Based off of Chapter 1 of my Upcoming Book (Unless it's Already Out) *The Powers of Ra!*

I've Created my Own Publishing Company, *Etched Mythos,* and this Graphic Novel is the First Book that Has Been Officially Published Under Its Name!

Writing This Second Book and Starting This Business Has Equally Been the Scariest, Most Frustrating, Expensive, Yet Coolest Thing I've Ever Done, and I Want to Produce More for Your Enjoyment as You Get Lost In my Characters.

Renetta Goes From Slave to "Goddess" in a Matter of Mere Moments, and When People Have Power, It Brings Out Who They Really Are. Renetta, and Especially Those Around Her, Will Learn Together what kind of Goddess She Will Be Over Egypt...

"Metakomik" is the Company I Outsourced to for the Illustrations and they Knocked it Out of the Park! As Another Thank You, I'd Like to Present Some StoryBoard Art For Some of my Favorite Pages From This Issue of the Story.

Once Again, Thank You For Reading, and For Being a Part in the Story of my Business.

SLAVE
GUARD
SLAVE
GUARD
GUARD
SLAVE
RENETTA
RENETTA

GUARD
RENETTA
GUARD
RENETTA
GUARD
SLAVE
GUARD
SLAVE
RENETTA

GUARD
GUARD
GUARD
RENETTA
RENETTA
RENETTA

SLAVE
GUARD

SLAVE

GUARD

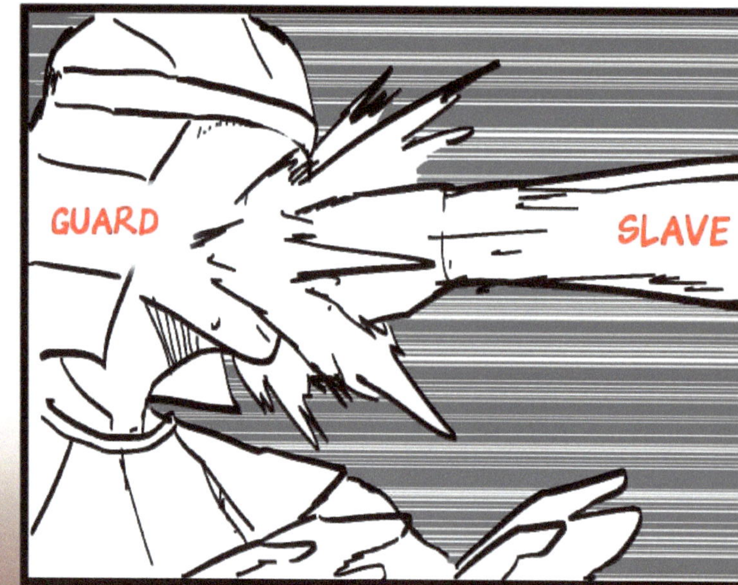
GUARD
SLAVE

RENETTA

RENETTA

REINETA
ANKHSET

ANKHSET

ANKHSET

ANKH SET

ANKH SET

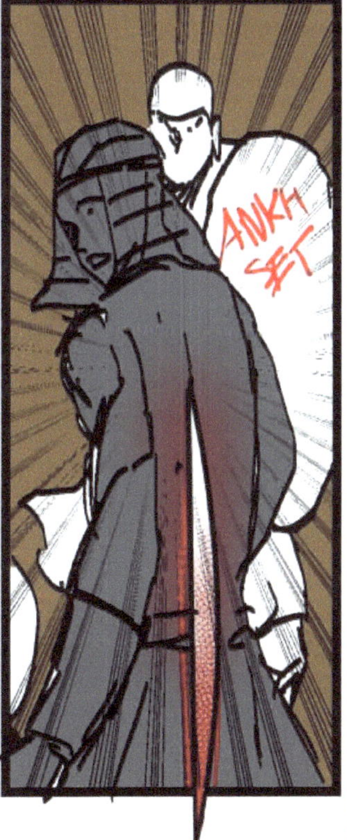

ANKH SET

ANKH SET
Guard

SLAVES
-ANKHSEA
WE TOOK
THE ADVENTAGE
WE WERE GIVEN.

ANHH-
SET
WE
TRIED....

-RENEFTA
SLAVES
-GUARD

THEY FEEL
THEY LOOM
LARGE
THEY DO
THEIR BEST
TO KEEP
US SMALL

BUT NOW, RA'S GIVEN ME
THE POWER TO BRING
THEM TO THEIR KNEES

The Powers of Ra
Story by :
Jared Burgess
Art by :
Metakomik